Minnie and Moo
Save the Earth

Denys Cazet

DK PUBLISHING, INC.

for Nancy Jackson
with affection
from the boys

DK

DK Publishing, Inc., 375 Hudson Street, New York, New York 10014
Visit us on the World Wide Web at http://www.dk.com
Text and illustrations copyright © 1999 by Denys Cazet

Library of Congress Cataloging-in-Publication Data
Cazet, Denys.
Minnie and Moo save the earth / by Denys Cazet. — 1st ed.
p. cm.
"A DK Ink book."
Summary: While relaxing in the farmer's hot tub,
two cow friends unknowingly thwart an alien invasion and save the planet.
ISBN-13: 978-0-7894-2594-2 (hc) ISBN-13: 978-0-7894-3929-1 (pbk)
[1. Cows—Fiction. 2. Extraterrestrial beings—Fiction. 3. Humorous stories.]
I. Title. PZ7.C2985Mm 1999 [Fic]—dc21 98-47394 CIP AC

The illustrations for this book were created with pencil and watercolor.
The illustration on these pages was drawn in pencil.
The text of this book is set in 18 point Berling.
Printed and bound in China
First edition, 1999
(hc)   10 9 8 7 6 5 4
(pbk) 10 9 8

1

Late One Night

Minnie and Moo

sat in the farmer's hot tub.

"This feels so good," said Minnie.

Moo stared into the night.

"I wonder if I should go on a diet,"

said Minnie. "I feel . . . beefy."

Moo wondered about the stars.

"I *am* big boned," added Minnie.

Moo wondered about the moon.

"Moo," said Minnie.

"Should I take up

the trampoline again?"

"What?" said Moo.

Minnie sighed.

"Moo, you haven't heard
a word I said!"

"Beefy!" said Moo. "You said beefy."

"Oh, Moo," said Minnie sadly.

"You have been thinking again."

"It was only a small think," said Moo.

Minnie shook her head.

"I was just wondering," said Moo.

"About the stars."

"Moo," said Minnie.

"Everyone knows that stars
are just little bags of gas
that go burp in the night."

"No," said Moo.

"I am wondering
about life on other planets.
Look at all those stars, Minnie.
We can't be the only
intelligent life in the universe."

A comet fell across the sky.

"Did you see that?" said Moo.

"It looked like it landed
on the hill.

Maybe it was a spaceship?

Maybe . . ."

Minnie looked at Moo.

"It was just a thought," said Moo.

"Exactly," said Minnie.

2

Inside the Spaceship

The lights in the spaceship dimmed.

"Up snooper scope,"

said the Captain.

"Well? Well? What do you see?"

"I see many trees and buildings,"

said Number One.

"What else?" said the Captain.

Number One pushed a button.

He saw a horse and two pigs.

"The creatures on this planet
are very big," said Number One.

"We are very small!"

"Nonsense!" yelled the Captain.

"Find their army!"

Number One turned a dial.

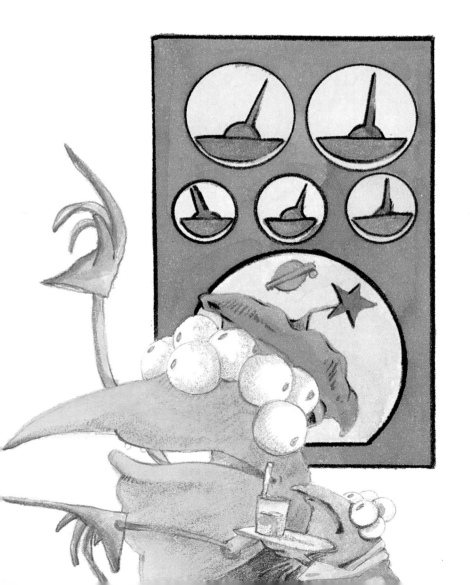

"Well?" said the Captain.

"I see two very large creatures," said Number One.

The Captain stopped pacing.

"What are they doing?"

"I think they are cooking."

"Cooking?"

"Boiling, sir . . .

and sir, they have weapons."

"Ray guns?"

"Horns!" said Number One.

"Better bring in the mother ship!"

said the Captain sadly.

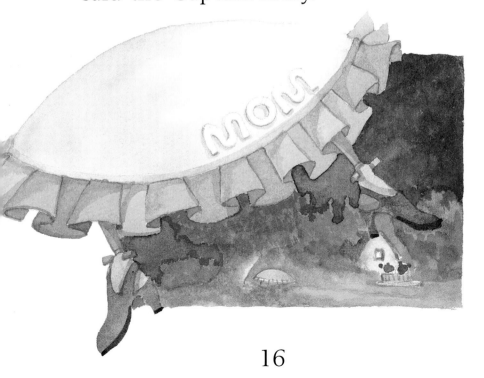

3

The Second Comet

Moo stood up.

She pointed at the hill.

"Minnie! Did you see that?"

Minnie looked around. "What?"

"Another comet," said Moo.

"It is landing in the same spot."

Minnie yawned.

"I guess I missed it," she said.

"Is my hair getting curly?"

Moo looked at Minnie.

"A little," said Moo.

Minnie rubbed the top of her head.

"Is it the steam," she wondered,

"or this new shampoo?"

18

Minnie stood up.

She wrapped a towel

around her head.

"Moo, look at you," she said.

"Your hair is standing straight up."

Minnie wrapped a towel

around Moo's head.

"It's this *shampoo!*" said Minnie.

A mosquito buzzed Moo.

She picked up the flyswatter.

WHAP!

"BUGS!" said Minnie.

"What pests!"

The farmer's dog began to bark.

It barked and barked.

The porch light went on.

The farmer opened the back door

and let the dog in.

The light went off.

4

The Mother Ship

The Mother General of the
mother ship waved her arms.
"This planet is nothing
but a green space pimple.
Don't you know
how to do your job, Captain?
What are you waiting for?"

"Look!" shouted Number One.

"They are standing up!"

"Giants!" gulped the Mother General.

"They have weapons!"

"What is that on their heads?"
asked the Captain.

"Helmets!" said the Mother General.

"You fools!

Don't you have eyes

on the top of your heads?"

she shouted.

"Don't you have ears on your bottoms?

That light was a signal.

That barking noise was an alarm.

They know we are here!

Number One . . .

call in the father ship!"

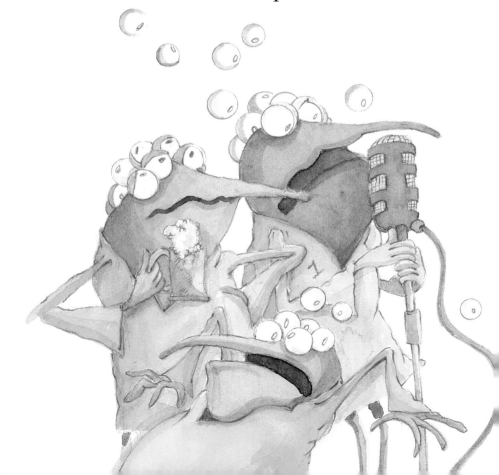

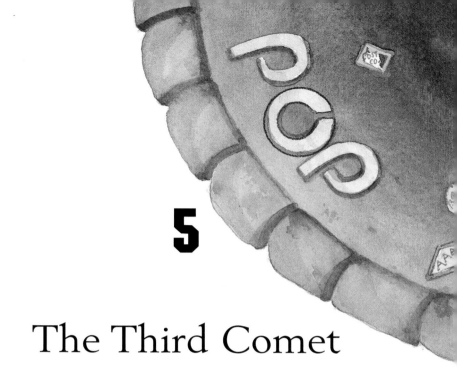

5

The Third Comet

Moo watched the third comet

fall from the sky.

"Minnie?" said Moo.

"I saw another one.

It landed in the same place."

Minnie sighed.

"That's nice," she said.

Moo stared at the top of the hill.

"There is something odd going on

up there," she said.

"Something about that tree."

Minnie reached over the side
of the hot tub
and picked up some crackers.
She put them on a dish
next to a piece of cheese.
"Try this," she said.
"This cheese is called brie.
It is my favorite."

Moo ate some cheese.

"It tastes best with this—

alfalfa fizz," said Minnie.

She filled their glasses.

"Mmm," said Moo.

"Minnie, I have been thinking."

"I never think," said Minnie proudly.

"I am much too busy."

"But, Minnie, there is something—"

"Moo," said Minnie.

"Turn up the jets a bit."

The hot tub bubbled.

"And the heat, too."

Steam rose into the night.

6

The Father Ship

Emperor Pop of the father ship
was angry.
"This planet should have been
shrink-wrapped and mailed
hours ago!" he shouted.
"What is the problem, Captain?
What is the problem, Mother General?

Why hasn't the attack begun?"

The Mother General pointed

at the snooper scope.

"They are big.

We are small.

They have weapons.

They have helmets.

We saw a signal.

We heard an alarm.

They are sitting in a spaceship.

They are eating something."

"Hmmm," said Emperor Pop.

"It must be the source of their power."

"Your Ugliness—LOOK!"

Everyone looked at the screen.

"Their spaceship!" said the Captain.

"It is bubbling."

Emperor Pop moaned.

"They know we are here!

Prepare for the invasion!"

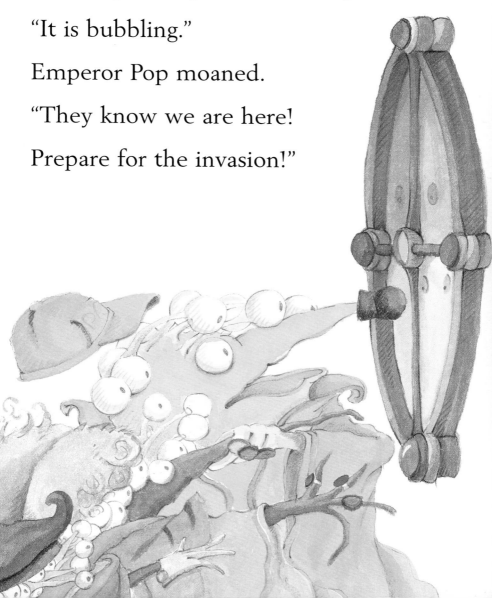

The hot tub hummed.

"They are preparing for takeoff,"
yelled the Mother General.

"Attack!" screamed Emperor Pop.

"Attack! Attack! Attack!"

7

The Invasion

They swarmed down the hill.

They buzzed over the hot tub.

They stung Minnie and Moo

with their ray guns.

"Ow!" said Moo.

"Ow!" said Minnie.

"These bugs are big!"

Moo picked up the flyswatter.

WHAP!

She swatted one.

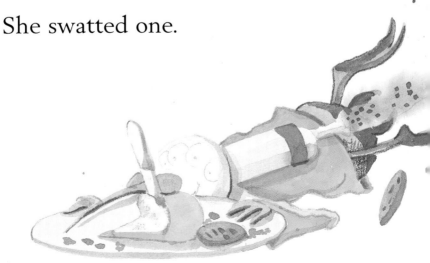

W_HA P! W_HAP!

W_HA_P!

She swatted three more.

"MINNIE!" Moo yelled.

"They're taking our cheese!"

"MY BRIE!" cried Minnie.

Minnie grabbed the flyswatter.

She leaped out of the hot tub.

W H *A* P !

"MY BRIE!" she shouted.

40

WHAP! WHAP! WHAP!

WHAP! WHAP!

"MY BRIE!

MY BRIE! MY BRIE!"

WHAP!   WHAP!   WHAP!

"You got them!" Moo cried.

"The rest are flying away!

WHAP!

W HAP!

WHAP!

W HAP!

WHAP!

Minnie, they're gone!

WHAP!   WHAP!

Minnie, STOP!

WHAP!

MINNIE!"

Moo took the flyswatter.

"They're gone," said Moo gently.

"Let's get back in the tub.

I don't want you to catch cold."

"I'm sorry," Minnie sobbed.

"I don't know what came over me."

"It's okay," said Moo. "They are gone."

"So is our cheese," sniffed Minnie.

8

Peace on Earth

A light glowed on the hill.

Suddenly, three comets

shot across the sky.

"Minnie! Did you see that?"

"What?"

Moo put her arm around Minnie.

"Nothing," she said.

Moo took the plate from Minnie.
She put more crackers on the plate
and added a new wedge of cheese.
"Surprise!" said Moo.

"Oh, Moo, thank you."

"This cheese is called

fromage de vache," said Moo.

"It was made by my aunt in France."

"Yum," said Minnie.

"Let's go to France tomorrow,"

said Moo. "It is just over the hill."

"How do you know?" Minnie asked.

"This morning," said Moo,

"I saw the farmer's wife

bring home a loaf of French bread."

"Really?" said Minnie.

Moo refilled their glasses.

"Really," she said.

The farm was quiet.

The world was calm.

"Cheers," said Minnie.

"Cheers," said Moo.

CLINK.